AF484417

PALE HORSE
PUBLICATIONS

CASUALTY OF WAR
U.S. MARSHAL SAM BASS

JOHN THURMOND

Cover Art by Michael Thomas
Cover design by Outlaws Publishing
Edited by Ann Mealler
Published by Outlaws Publishing
April 2021
10987654321

Chapter One

My name John Harris and I want to share my story with you. The real story of how I became Sam Bass, U.S. Marshal.

My earliest childhood memory is of some nuns cooking griddle cakes on an old woodburning stove. The smoke was burning my eyes and I was crying, but I couldn't tell the cook that as I had not yet learned to talk. The nuns were talking about the Civil War being over and wondering what they were going to do with all the orphaned kids that kept showing up at the doors.

I hadn't learned how to talk very well, but I could understand what they were saying. I must have been two, maybe a little younger, at the time. I remember it vividly because I got swatted for crying. That made me very mad and it wasn't long that I learned how to talk, determined that I would never happen again.

I never remembered anyone ever leaving the orphanage, just more kids arriving all the time. I had a favorite that was warm and made me feel good in the winter. When I outgrew it, I saw it on another kid that was smaller than me. I guess it became his favorite shirt. It seemed like that shirt went on forever, never getting to leave that building.

On sunny days, the older boys got to go up on the roof and play. It had a tall fence around it. Mainly, we just dreamed of going outside and into the streets. Me and another boy named Bob Ford always played together. Bob wanted to be a bank robber when he got older. He always told me that when we got old enough, the nuns would kick us out in the street and we had to find a job and another place to live because we would never be able to come back to the orphanage.

Bob figured the best way to earn a lot of money was to rob a bank. It sounded like a good plan to me, so we practice robbing each other. We made ourselves some guns out of wood and hid them in our pockets. We robbed each other every chance we got. Of course, all we ever had was paper money we made ourselves, cut out of old newspapers we'd found in the nuns' room.

Bob jumped me one day in the staircase between the floors, beat me up, and robbed me of my money. I gave him a cussing and one of the nuns overheard me. I got sent to the head nun's office. The nuns at the orphanage always called me John. It was the only name I ever knew. I never had a last name until I was around fifteen years old.

Me and the other boys were never allowed to leave the orphanage. It was just a big, cold building somewhere in St. Louis, Missouri. We sat in a classroom and learned how to read and write, and a little math. We had a hot bath once a week.

Sometimes us boys would sneak up on the roof in warmer weather and watch freight wagons and people moving up and down the street. I could see out past the last building of town if I stood up on the chimney top. I wondered what was out there. I'd read about Indians and outlaws in a Dime Novel I found in the hallway one summer.

Me and Bob Ford always hung out together. Sometimes we would play cowboys and Indians when we weren't practicing robbing each other. Bob was a little older than I was.

The nuns let us build a pigeon coop on the roof one summer. We fed the pigeons dried bread left over from the kitchen. One day I threw a dead bird off the roof and it hit a horse on its rump. That caused a wreck and a lot of excitement. My backside got warmed up for that.

It got to the point where me and several other boys had to start sleeping on the floor because there were not enough beds for the younger boys. And, at dinner my bowl used to be full. Now, it was only half full or half empty, no matter how you looked at it. That went on like that for several years. The place was crowded. No one ever got adopted out that I remember, just new kids showing up all the time.

One spring, it must have been April, I was fourteen and Bob must have been fifteen. Some men came around and put paper tags on us. They were little round white paper tags with a shiny metal edge around it. They were tied through a button hole on our shirts with a strong string that had a number and a name on it. All mine had on it was the name John and it said, 'casualty of the Civil War', and my birth date of May 13, 1864. I'd never known that before.

My friend, Bob Ford, told me it was a Friday. He was older than me but I never understood why he made such a big deal out of Friday. Anyway, the men gave us new clothes and shoes and marched us outside and down to the rail station. That was about twenty blocks away—I kept count. I figured I needed to in case I needed to find my way back to the orphanage.

"This is the day, John," Bob said as we marched along the street. "They're kicking us out of the orphanage. As soon as the men leave us alone, let's jump a policeman, get us gun and rob a bank so we'll have some real money."

Of course, the men never left us alone. They loaded us all on some old box cars down by the railroad track. There was straw on the floors and they smelled to high heaven. It took some getting used to. We learned later on they were cattle cars. The railroad used them to move cows in. They crowded at least forty of us boys, twelve and older, in a car and locked the doors. We figured they didn't want us to escape.

I counted five cars in all, full of kids. The girls were loaded into a different kind of car that had the word "pullman" on the side of it. The first car had the girls in it, the rest of them had boys. A lot of them were younger and crying because they had no idea of what was going to happen.

As soon as the last car was loaded the train started moving. It was the first time I'd ever been out of the orphanage. Bob and some of the older boys said they were going to kick us out of the box car when we left town and were out in the countryside. I was thinking for sure that I was going to starve to death or some Indian would scalp me.

"What's out there?" I asked Bob.

"No streets and no buildings," Bob told me. "Just open country."

I never saw open country before so I watched until I got tired, then finally laid down and went to sleep.

The train stopped in every town we came to. Men and women would crowd around the train and point to a child, then the men who had taken us would throw the chosen kid off the train. It finally dawned on me they were adopting us out. I'd never seen a kid get adopted out before, just new ones arriving at the orphanage all the time.

I made it all the way to Denton, Texas. I knew that because there was a big sign along the tracks just before the train stopped at the depot. There weren't many of us left in the box car I was in. Finally, an older man and woman picked me out. They looked me over, felt my arm and leg muscles, counted my fingers and looked at my teeth.

"We'll take him," the man said.

They signed some papers, loaded me up in their buggy, and drove me home with me bouncing around in the back like a sack of potatoes. I had no idea what was fixing to happen to me, but I remembered that I never told my friend Bob goodbye. I never told anybody goodbye before.

When we arrived at their farm, the man said his name was James Harris. The woman was Hattie. It must have been around noon because the sun was over my head. James showed me a bed out in the hay barn up in the loft. He told me the stalls were for the horses and it was my job to keep them cleaned. He showed me how he wanted it done. There was hay in the manger and a water tank out back that had a windmill by it with a pipe running to the tank. James showed me how to turn it on by releasing the brake and said the wind would make it turn.

"Keep it full," he told me, "or I'll whoop your backside. Wash yourself off in the horse tank every day. If Hattie ever smells you, she won't let you eat in the house. And no cursing or Hattie will wash you mouth out with lye soap."

I knew what that was all about. I gave Bob a cussing one time for something he did to me and them nuns liked to have drowned me in soapy water.

James told me breakfast was at daybreak, the noon meal was when Hattie rang the bell on the porch, and there'd be dried bread for supper.

Hattie showed me how to gather the eggs and milk the cow the next day. I worked every day except Sunday. Of course, you still had to milk the cow. Then we'd get cleaned up and go to church.

It went on like that all summer. When the first light snow fell Hattie let me stay in the house at night. She told me it was her son's room, that he'd went off to the Civil War and never came back home. Hattie said she never knew what had happened to him. That was the first time in my life I had a room to myself, and a last name. John Harris.

I got two new suits of clothes and boots twice a year, one to wear while the others were being washed. I thought I was rich. And I was, compared to what I'd had in the orphanage.

By the time I was sixteen I knew how to ride a horse and plow. They only had about twenty acres for grazing and a garden for Hattie. I was as happy as a newborn puppy until Hattie took sick and passed away a couple of years later.

Old man Harris got meaner than hell after that and took to whooping me with a belt when anything got broken or did not go the way he wanted it to. I made up my mind, lying in bed one night, that I was leaving. I knew he would run me down and whip me good if he caught me so I figured I had to come up with a plan.

I thought about it for a month or more and, come late spring, I put that plan to work. I told James I was going to sleep in the barn because the house was getting warm at night. Around two in the morning I saddle the only riding horse we had, got out the buggy wrench and took all the wheel nuts off the buggy wheels and threw them in the horse trough. I figured if James lit out after me, he wasn't going very far before all the wheels came off the buggy.

James had an old Yellow Boy Henry rimfire 44/40 rifle hanging in the barn. We used it for skunks when they got in the chicken pen. I checked it for shells and the old gun was full. I slipped it into the scabbard under the saddle, made me a bedroll with a ground tarp wrapped around it, and spent an hour cutting up some dried beef and salt-cured ham that James kept hanging in the barn. I stuffed my saddle bags full of dried meat, slipped up on the porch and stole an old frying pan that Hattie kept there to feed her dog in. I tied it all on my bedroll and left the farm behind me, headed southwest. I'd heard tell it was warmer that direction.

That danged old dog was following his pan, so me and Sam (that's what Hattie called him) left the farm and James behind. James had heard me when I sneaked up on the porch and got Sam's pan and wondered about it for some time until he heard a horse walking up the gravel drive to our house. When he got up and seen I was gone with his saddle horse, he hitched up the buggy and took out after me, thinking he was going to give me a thrashing I would remember the rest of my life. That was about the time when all the wheels came off the buggy at once. The noise scared his horse and it stampeded. There was no stopping that horse until he wore himself or the buggy came apart.

I walked that old saddle horse nearly all the way to town before I heard a loud noise behind me and a lot of curse words. I took to the brush alongside the road and watched as old man Harris came by in the buggy with no wheels, the horse dragging him along with buggy bed on the ground. I almost broke out laughing aloud at the sight, but held my breath until he was long past. I followed him close to a half mile farther on and came to a road sign that read, "Decatur, West; Fort Worth, South." I could tell James was headed to Decatur from the skid marks on the road, so I headed south to Fort Worth, Texas. I'd never been there before, but knew I would be the next day. The sign said it was forty miles to Fort Worth and I didn't think you could drag a buggy that far and it not come apart. And, the buggy horse wasn't saddle broken, so old man Harris was going to have to walk and lead the horse back home.

Chapter Two

"Wow!" I was thinking to myself. Fort Worth, Texas was a big town and I needed to find myself a job. I wandered all over the place and finally wound up at the stock yards. A man there by the name of Henry Jones told me I could help load cows in them box cars and sleep in the hay barn along with my horse and dog. He made sure to tell me there was no smoking in the hay barn and I told him I never smoked and never planned to. Tobacco smelled too bad to me. I did not like it or the smell of it.

I told Henry I needed to get paid every day because I had no idea when I might have to leave town. He looked at me and asked if I was a runaway. I told him about old man Harris getting mean after Hattie passed away.

"Okay," he said. "Happens sometimes. I ran away from home myself when I was just a youngster."

So there it was. I had a job and a place to sleep. I ate out of my saddle bags for a month and saved up my money. I found a place where I could get a meal for five cents and I was getting paid a dollar a day. It wasn't long before I had close to a hundred dollars on me. I split the leather on my boot tops and hit a lot of it, sewed it closed.

Late one week I saw James Harris prowling around town and decided it was time I left. I saddle my old horse and me and Sam left, headed south. It wasn't long before we made it to Waco, Texas. We darn near drowned trying to cross the Brazos River. It was high water. Must have rained upstream. Well, at least I was clean as I took me a bath trying to cross that river. The sun was so hot I dried out real fast.

I was hungry and my belly was growling at me, so I tied my horse up in front of a cantina just across the street from the sheriff's office. It was a big place called Rosa's, that had a big sign over the boardwalk. I saw to the water trough then walked up to the batwing doors.

Most cantinas had dried beef or ham and you could build yourself a sandwich for a nickel, and a warm beer for a penny. Old Sam was trying to follow me in and I told him no and pointed to a post in front of my horse. Old Sam laid down and went to sleep after getting himself a drink along with my horse.

I walked into the cantina. It was very dark inside. I waited just inside the doors for my eyes to adjust to the room when I heard Sam growl. I turned around just in time to see a man kick Sam into the street, and he was limping on one of his back legs. I stepped out on the porch as the man was pulling his pistol and shot old Sam dead.

I walked up behind that man and kicked him in his left knee as hard as I could, truing to break it. I must have succeeded because down he went. He dropped his gun on the boardwalk and it bounced into the street. He was trying to get up on the boardwalk and kept falling because his knee gave out on him. He called me a bad name and I kicked him out into the street. Then I followed him. He was covered in dust and he tried to get up again by grabbing ahold of my saddle strap. I waited until he was full up on one leg and kicked him in the groin as hard as I could. He lost his lunch and passed out right there in the street.

Now, I had grown a lot since leaving the orphanage. I'd gained seventy-five pounds, not a bit of it fat. It put me close to two hundred ten pounds. And I was nearly six feet tall. I had a fight every week when I was in the orphanage with Bob Ford or some other older boy so I had learned how to take care of myself early in life. Our motto at the orphanage was take no prisoners. Of course, we never hurt anybody, but this was different. This man had shot and killed Sam and I wasn't going to let it pass without retribution.

The sheriff showed up. A man named Mack Boyles. He told me he'd seen the whole thing; that feller tried to push my dog off the porch and when Sam growled at him, he kicked the dog off the boardwalk and shot him.

"You were a little rough on him, boy," Mack said.

"My name's John Harris," I told him.

"Well, John Harris, let's look this feller over and see how much damage you done to him," the sheriff said.

"Looks like he may never walk again without a stick to help himself."

I helped Mack drag the feller over to the jail across the street.

"Let's put him in a cell just in case he gets rowdy when he wakes up," Mack suggested.

Sure as my name was John, the man threw a fit when he woke up in jail and realized he might never walk again without a stick to lean on. He called me and Mack a lot of words I had never heard before. Mack stared at the man and never said a word, just walked over to his desk and started going through wanted posters.

I watched for a spell and picked up one of the posters before Mack got to it.

"I believe this is the man we locked up, Mack," I told the sheriff, then started reading the poster aloud. "David Harold. Blonde hair that looks like a newborn chicken. He should have called himself Amarillo Perro, Spanish for Yellow Dog. Even his beard is cropped short. Everything matches along with his height, weight and blue eyes. Twenty-five hundred dollar reward, dead or alive, for bank robbery and killing a teller over in Temple, Texas."

"Damn," Mack said. "I had him right here in town and never knew it until you kicked him into the street. Looks like you earned yourself some cash. The state of Texas put up the reward money, so I'll get you paid in the morning. The Judge will have to sign off on the payment."

I told Mack I was buying supper and invited him to come along. He locked up the jail and we walked to the café. I spent the night in a hotel room that cost me double. I wondered about that some but finally went to sleep. I got a bath and new clothes the next day, and my first shave and haircut in a barber shop. I liked the way I felt and decided to make it a habit.

I collected my reward that morning. After the judge paid me and I was walking back toward the jail, I handed Mack a hundred dollars.

"You don't have to do that," Mack said. "You caught him."

"I know," I told him, "but you locked him up and I was just going to leave him in the street."

"Well, okay," said Mack as he folded the money and put it in his shirt pocket. "Go catch some more bad men."

I stopped in the street and looked at Mack. "Is it legal for me to go after a wanted man?" I asked him.

"Yes," Mack told me, "as long as you catch the right man and don't make the mistake of killing an innocent one. Let me give you something for this money. Follow me over to the jail."

Mack gave me an old Colt 45 that still had some bluing left on it, with a pearl handle and a heavy leather holster on a wide belt. The belt had loops on it for ten shells. The old gun had a scar on the left side of the barrel. It looked like someone had tried to brand it. I asked Mack what it was.

"A lightning strike," Mack replied. "The cowboy that owned it was shooting up the town after getting drunk one Saturday night. He was out in the street and it had just started to rain. He pointed the gun up in the air and just as he fired the last shell, lightning struck the barrel and killed him. This old gun and five dollars was all he had on him when we buried him up on Boot Hill last spring." He handed me the gun and said, "Get yourself a could hundred rounds of ammunition and learn how to use it the right way."

"What's the right way, Mack?" I asked.

"Never fan your first shot," he answered. "Make it count. Take your time. Just because you're a fast draw doesn't mean a dam thing in a gun fight. Keep yourself calm and be a good shot. That's the only advice I can give you. Just be the last man standing and never carry more than five rounds in that old Colt. The hammer spur will sit on a live round if you do, and if you bump the hammer, it will go off and shoot your toes off. Keep an empty chamber under the hammer all the time."

With that said, I left and walked over to the hardware store where I bought five hundred rounds and a cleaning kit. I needed to clean my old Yellow Boy and the Colt. I rode out to a mesa and set up camp. I fired a hundred rounds that first day and spent most of the night learning how to fast-draw and cock the Colt without it going off by accident and shooting my toes off. It took me close to a week to learn and it wasn't easy. I fired close to four hundred rounds before I really got used to the gun and could hit a target without really trying to. I found out I could hit a tin plate at fifty feet without really aiming, just draw and shoot.

I decided I needed to go back into town. I'd shot too many holes in my tin plate, not the smartest thing I'd ever don, and I needed a new one and more shells. I visited Mack and asked if I could have copies of his wanted posters.

"Sure," Mack said, "I've got copies of nearly all of them."

There were twenty-five in all. I studied them that night in my room, where I still had to pay double. I spent the next day watching people. As sure as the sun was shining, I spotted someone from one of Mack's posters. His name was Dan Holloway. I followed him into the cantina. If I'd remembered right, he was wanted for burning down a hay barn. The warrant was out of Dallas, Texas, with a five hundred dollar bounty, alive. I followed him inside where he bellied up to the bar and ordered himself a shot of whiskey.

I watched him as he went to pick up the whiskey glass and, just before he did, I said, "Dan Holloway? Man, I haven't seen you in a coon's age."

He turned and I stuck my right hand out to shake hands with him. As soon as he took my hand, I hit him with a left hook and knocked him silly. Then I spun him around and pulled his gun out if its holster. I kicked him out on the boardwalk and into the street. I shoved his gun into his face and told him to walk as I pointed to the sheriff's office.

I was surprised Mack was still at his desk. I told him I had Dan Holloway and Mack locked him up. I collected another payday and gave Mack fifty dollars.

"What's this for?" asked Mack when I gave him the money.

"For the good advice," I replied with a grin.

After breakfast the next day, the weather was warm and sunny. I was enjoying the day just walking around town. As I passed the jail I saw two kids, a boy and a girl around six or seven years old. They were sitting on the boardwalk in front of the jail and it looked like they had been crying. I stopped and asked what was wrong.

"My pop got locked up," the boy said. "We was just passing through town going to our new ranch out in New Mexico Territory. My mom got if from her father after he passed away last winter. We ain't never going to get there now." The boy started crying again.

I walked into the jail to see who he was talking about but the only man Mack had locked up was Dan

Holloway. Mack was gone so I walked back outside and asked the boy what his last name was.

"Holloway," the boy answered.

"Damn," I thought. I'd upset someone's plans for a happy life.

I went back inside and looked for the cell keys. I found them and started to unlock the door when it dawned on me that Mack was going to know someone had let Holloway out. So, I took the key, made an outline of it on paper, folded it and hit in in my pocket. I asked Dan why he had burned down that barn. He told me it was an accident but the barn had belonged to the local judge who filed charges against him ten years earlier. I just turned around an left.

I'd seen an old blacksmith shop at the edge of town that wasn't being used. It was next to an old shack. I walked out there and saw an old woman sitting on the porch of the shack. I asked her if she owned the blacksmith shop. She said her husband had, but he'd passed away the year before. I asked her if I could use it for the rest of the day and that I was willing to pay her.

"How much?" she asked.

"Ten dollars," I said.

"Use it all week for that much," she told me.

I paid her and went to work. The orphanage I was raised up in had a shop in the basement. I had used about all the tools there at one time or another. By sunset I had me a key and was pretty sure it would work. I wrapped it up in paper with a note inside that said, "Get your family out of Waco, Texas tonight and don't ever come back. And take the key with you."

After cleaning myself up and having had my evening meal, I watched Mack and his deputies. They always walked the streets between eleven and midnight. I knew Mack always took the jail key with him on rounds. Right after eleven, I threw the key I'd made into the window, right into Dan Holloway's cell. Then I hid across the street to see if the man would leave. I hadn't been in hiding but a minute when Dan walked out of the jail and disappeared down an alley. I silently hoped he would make it to New Mexico. I made up my mind right then that if I was going to be a bounty hunter, I was going to be damned careful from now on about which ones I went after. It would be bad men only, no more petty crimes.

Chapter Three

I stayed around Waco until later in the fall then finally headed southeast to warmer weather. Sheriff Mack and his boys were still trying to figure out when I left how Dan Holloway had escaped from the jail when Mack had the keys on himself. They talked about it all the time.

I decided to just leave Waco. I'd heard there were a lot of wanted men running up and down the Mississippi River on river boats, so I thought I'd like to ride on one myself.

I was about to give up on ever seeing a river boat when I arrived in Baton Rouge. I was sitting on my old horse when a man getting off a boat asked me where he could buy a horse and saddle. I told him for five hundred dollars he could have mine.

The fellow looked my old horse over and said, "Okay," then pulled out five hundred dollars in gold coins. I got my Yellow Boy and saddle bags, handed him the reins to James Harris' old horse and saddle, scratched my name on a handmade bill of sale, and walked to the river.

I found the river boat captain and asked him if he was headed south to New Orleans, and I bought myself a ticket. The captain wouldn't rent me a room and I wondered about that some. So, I slept on the upper deck

one night and the lower deck the next. We arrived in
New Orleans the following evening.

I'd never seen nothing like New Orleans before. There
was so much moss hanging off the trees. It nearly
touched the ground in some places. There were a lot of
big old houses up and down the river bank. They all had
big posts on the front porches. I saw one that was three
windows tall and had live oak trees planted along the
road on each side. It looked too rich for me to visit.

I bought myself a new set of clothes, had a bath and a
shave. Later that evening I found myself visiting several
bars along a street named Bourbon. I found out they
don't call them cantinas in Mississippi, just bars. It must
have been a river boat thing because if you got hung up
in the river, it was on something called a sand bar. I
guess in town it was just bar you got hung up in.

I was walking down a red cobblestone street late in
the evening. There was a cool wind blowing off the water
and piano music coming out of several of them bars. I
was thinking that I was really going to like this town. I
saw a bar with a chicken hanging over the entrance. It
had great big red painted batwing doors. I wondered
about it as I walked on past it. Then, for some reason, I
turned around and walked back to it. I stood there a while
and finally walked inside. The chicken whose head was
missing looked like one of them fighting chickens, just
hanging there over the batwing doors. A young woman
was sitting at a table playing some kind of a card game

all by herself. She had green bird feathers tied in her long hair, big, dark eyes, light brown skin, long gold earrings that nearly touched her shoulders, and a red dress that went all the way to the floor. She had a white shawl around her shoulders and was a darn good looking woman, I thought.

She was sitting at a table with cards scattered out in front of her. When she looked up and saw me she screamed, in French, "Quitee cet endroit maintenant que chose de mal est entre' dans la pi'ece," (leave this place now, something evil has entered the room).

Now, one of the nuns at the orphanage I was raised in spoke French, so I kind of knew what the woman had shouted at me. I had no idea if she mean me, but every person in the bar left in a hurry except or me. I had no idea she was talking about me. I learned later it was Creole French and she was the Voodoo queen of New Orleans.

People leaving the bar had pushed me farther into the room as they were running out the batwing doors. The woman rose from her table like a ghost, very quiet and smooth. She walked around me twice with a chicken leg in her hand and touched me in several places. She finally stopped at my old Colt and said, "Place it on the table and remove the bullets."

After I finished, she sat down across from me, took her chicken leg, and rolled them bullets across the table one at a time. Then, she started in on the old Colt pistol. She ran that chicken leg up and down the right side.

"Your name is John," she said rather than asked.

"Yes," I told her.

"It is written under here," she said, pointing at the grips.

I told her I had never put my name under there. She looked at me and I kind of felt funny.

"It is written," was all she said. Then she turned it over and saw the scar on the barrel from the lightning strike Mack had told me about. "Mal fle'au," she said.

"What?" I asked.

"Evil this gun is," she said. "It will consume you, John, if you let it." then she asked me if I'd ever killed anyone with it. I told her no, only a tin plate and some rocks.

"If you point this gun at anyone it will go off by itself," she warned. "It has a mind of its own. Be very careful who you point it at because they will be killed. Very evil, this gun is. Take it and yourself out of here now."

When she got up to leave the room I asked what her name was.

Marie Laveau was the name she said, and she seemed to float across the room. I reloaded my old Colt and left after placing a silver dollar on the table.

Walking out the doors of the bar, I ran into the local law. A marshal by the name of Fetes Butler. He'd been out on the street and saw all the people run out of the bar. I asked him about Marie Laveau and he told me to stay away from her.

"She's an evil person that will put a spell on you that will last forever, and then on to your kids if you make her mad," he warned.

"Okay," was all I said. I asked him about wanted men with a bounty on their heads.

"Not allowed in Louisiana," Fetes said, "you must be from Texas. That's the only place where bounty hunting is allowed. Don't try it here or you will land yourself in jail."

"I'm heading upriver this evening," I assured him.

"Good," the marshal said, then turned and walked away.

Well, that was settled. Bounty hunting was not allowed so I needed to leave New Orleans or find myself another way to make a living. And, I sure didn't want to make Marie Laveau mad at me. I got into enough trouble on my own without a spell being put on me.

I bought myself a ticket all the way to Memphis, Tennessee on a flat-bottom river boat that had a big wheel behind it, paddling the water. Going upriver, I still couldn't get the captain to rent me a room, so I slept on the deck.

The river boat had some gamblers on it. I'd never played cards before, but I was a fast learning. For just a nickel and dime you could play all day and not lose a dollar. It was a good way to pass the time. It was either throw a hook in the water or gamble.

The last day on the river, the men got to betting more than they should have. One man got real mad at me for winning five dollars in a pot and he started cussing me out. He jumped up from the table and pulled his gun from a shoulder holster under his coat. I was still sitting down but my old Colt seemed to jump into my hand and it went off. Blew a big hole in that man, right in his mid-section. The other men at the table cleaned out his pockets and threw him overboard. Under he went, and on down the river.

I sat there with my eyes as big as silver dollars. No one said a word. We just kept on playing cards. But, I noticed the rest of the day the other men seemed to be afraid of me. They were saying 'yes sir' and 'no sir' when I asked them anything. "Damn," I was thinking. "Old Marie Laveau may be right about this old Colt. I ain't ever going to point this thing at anyone else again."

After leaving the river at Memphis I counted up my loose money. I had made five dollars on the river boat ride from New Orleans to Memphis, Tennessee. I had to pay six hundred dollars for a good horse and saddle at the livery barn. The horse was as black as midnight and had one white sock on his left back leg.

I stayed around Memphis for a week to learn that the law was hunting for anyone that rode the last river boat upriver from New Orleans. Seemed like the local law officer was missing and he was supposed to have been on the river boat. I made up my mind to ride for Fort Smith, Arkansas.

I decided I needed to change my appearance, so I bought a new outfit. It was all black, from the new black hat with a silver band, to the boots. I even had my gun belt and saddle dyed black at the local saddle shop. I figured if I was riding in the dark you could not have seen me if you was looking right at me. I kind of liked that look. I heard there was a Federal Judge over at Fort Smith, Arkansas, who was hiring men who could use a gun to control some place called the Indian Territory.

I left Memphis the next day. I took a ferry west across the Mississippi River. The man running the ferry told me the law in Memphis was hunting a man named John Harris for a shootout that happened on a river boat.

"Very fast with a gun, and a bad man, the way I heard tell," the man said.

I never said a word, just paid the man his dime for the ferry ride. After I'd paid my dime and walked my horse off the ferry, the man on the boat said, "The law in Tennessee can't chase you into Arkansas."

I never said a word, I just rode off west toward Fort Smith. "Damn," I was thinking, "I'm going to have to change my name."

I thought about it all the way. It took me a week to reach Fort Smith, Arkansas. I got myself a bath and shave, and told the barber to shave my head, that I was tired of long hair and thought it might be easier to keep my hat on in a high wind. Heck, it wasn't like I was going to sunburn anyway.

After a night in the livery barn, I made my way to the courthouse looking for this Federal Judge. I believe I'd heard his name was Isaac Parker.

Chapter Four

Fort Smith, Arkansas was a funny town. A man at the diner told me that I would have to eat outside. What the heck? I'd had a bath two days ago, but I didn't argue. I had my meal out under a shade tree. There was a big bench there so it wasn't bad. I kind of enjoyed it. I just left my plate and cup on the bench. Let the cook come get it.

I made my way to the courthouse. Looking around inside I found a door with Judge Isaac Parker's name on it. The judge was sitting behind a big desk with his feet propped up on it.

He looked at me over his glasses, "What do you want, boy?" he asked.

"I'm looking for a job," I said. "Heard you was hiring men to patrol the territory west of here."

I noticed the judge was looking at a telegram and saw that it had my name on it. John Harris.

"What's your name, boy?" the judge asked.

I never stuttered a bit. "Sam Bass," I said. It was the only name I could think of real fast. My old dog's name was Sam and a new kind of fish I'd eaten at Memphis and kind of liked, Bass.

"Let me see your gun, boy," the judge said.

As I pulled it out, I got the same kind of feeling we boys used to get when we scooted out feet across the wool rug in front of the Head Nun's office when we got called in for something we done wrong back in the orphanage. When you touched the door knob, it would leave a tingle on your fingers. Well, I got that same feeling from the old Colt's grips in the palm of my hand and nearly dropped it.

But, I held on and laid it on the desk in front of Judge Parker. He picked it up, took a screw driver from his desk drawer, removed the Pearl handle grips on the left side and looked on the back of it. "Clean," he said. He put the left grip back on and did the same thing to the one on the right. "Most men write their names under the grips," he said as he put the gun back together. As sure as I had a bath the day before, the name Sam Bass was written there in black carbon pencil.

I could not talk for a second. I just stood there, looking dumb and hoping my tongue wasn't hanging out. I said a silent 'thank you' to Marie Laveau.

"Well, Judge Parker said, "I thought you might be this John Harris they're looking for over in Memphis." He put my gun back together and handed it to me.

"Can you hit anything with it, Sam Bass?"

"Yeah, I can," I managed to say.

Judge Parker walked over to the window, looked across the yard at his gallows and asked if I could see the bell hanging between the nooses.

"Yeah," I told him. It must have been two hundred feet. A damn long shot for a Colt 45. I just yanked it out and fired, never bothered to aim. The bullet took a chunk of metal off the Judge's bell.

The judge walked back over his desk and began reading a letter. "Well," he said after a while, "this letter gives me the authority to hire U.S. Marshals to control the Indian Territory. It don't say they can't be black. Were your parents slaves?"

"No," I said. "I was raised in an orphanage and never knew them."

"Okay, Sam Bass," said the judge, "I'm going to hire you but you need to understand that I want every man you arrest brought in here alive. And, you need to understand that sometimes it's a two hundred mile trip to get them here. You'll get two hundred dollars a month plus your expenses. You will have to keep up with them yourself and turn them in at the end of every month. Any reward money is yours to keep. It may say dead or alive on the wanted poster, but I want them brought in here alive. It won't bother me if they're shot up, just as long as as they're alive when they get here."

With that said, Judge Isaac Parker swore me into service and pinned a silver badge on me that read, "U.S. Marshal."

"What are my orders?" I asked Parker.

"Just hang around town for now. Find you a place to live with a kitchen. People around here are kind of funny."

"Yeah, I know," I told him. I'd already found that out.

Judge Parker was thinking as I left, "Maybe this black man can get along better with the Indians than them other twelve white marshals I have." He wrote into the pay ledger, "Sam Bass, U.S. Marshal, badge number thirteen.

Wandering around time, I found myself a small house for sale for six hundred dollars. It was located by a creek with running water, had a small barn out back, and a split rail fence that went all the way down, across the creek and back.

I spent two nights awake, trying to figure out how to get my new job done without getting myself killed. The following day, I went to the hardware store and bought myself a big ten gauge, double-barreled shotgun. I had the blacksmith saw it off to around ten inches and weld a ring on the bottom of the right barrel. I bought myself a buggy like the one old man Harris had back in Texas, and built myself a box on the back with a door and padlock. It had one hole, just big enough to slip water and food through.

I was all set when I got word from Parker to go to the Nation's and pick up a man for a killing at the trading post in Checotah, Oklahoma. I studied the maps in Parker's office. It looked to be a long ride.

I set out with my saddle horse tied on to the back, and a double team on my buggy just in case one had trouble. I had oats and water for the horses and dried beef for myself.

It took five days to find the place. Most of the Indians I met were friendlier to me than white folks were. I kind of liked it. The lawman in Checotah was a young Indian who called himself Little Elk. He had a white man locked up in a wooden-barred jail in a shack that he called his office.

A lot of men were standing in the street, all hollering for the sheriff to turn the man loose because he was white and had only killed an Indian. It seemed they figured it was a legal killing and an Indian had no right to lock up a white man. Anyway, they got really upset when they saw me, a black man with a U.S. Marshal badge on. I think I kind of scared them some when I pointed my shotgun at them. I thought for a minute I was going to have to shoot my way into the jail. Good thing I'd brought my sawed off shotgun with me, loaded up with double ought buckshot.

The sun hadn't been up long when I got there. Little Elk was excited and told me that if I hadn't shown up when I did, he was just going to turn the man loose.

"How you figuring to get him out of here without killing some of his friends?" Little Elk asked me.

"I'll show you," I said. I asked the man to turn around in his cell. When he did, I thumped him on the head with my Colt. He was out cold. I rolled him over onto his belly, shoved my double barreled gun up under the back of his head, and ran a belt through the ring at the end of the barrel. I pulled the belt tight around his neck, then removed his belt and ran it around the stock and through the trigger guard. Then I ran it back around him and pulled it tight with the buckle in the back. Then I stood him up because it was about time for him to come to.

There he stood with a belt around his neck, keeping the gun aimed at the back of his head, and his own belt keeping the gun in the middle of his back. I had me a long leather string and tied it tow the triggers, then pulled both hammers back. The man wanted to know what he had tied to his back and around his neck. I told it about the sawed off shotgun.

I never bothered to tie his hands, just told him to walk and pushed him out the door and into all his friends standing in the street. I told them to look real good because if I pulled on the string, their friend was going to Hell real fast. Then I told them I was taking him to Fort Smith for a trial.

I told the man to climb into the box and I closed the door.

"Put your hands out the window," I told him. I handcuffed him with some irons the Judge had sent with me. I ran that leather string around the buggy, got up in the seat, and left Checotah for Fort Smith, Arkansas.

Some of the outlaw's friends followed me until around midnight. I stopped under some trees next to a creek and let the horses drink their fill. I tied the buggy to a tree and sneaked back the way I'd come on foot. I remembered the judge telling me any man he sent me after better come in alive. But, I didn't remember him saying anything about a man's friends.

It wasn't long until they came walking along, real quiet-like, trying to catch me napping. There were four of them riding real slow.

"You boys want to go home, or to Hell?" I asked as I stepped out in front of them.

"I'm going to send your black hide to Hell right now!" one of them said.

My old Colt jumped into my hand and bucked four times. When the smoke cleared, four men were dead. I collected their guns and tied their horses behind the buggy. I hitched up the team and headed on towards Fort Smith.

I stopped before daybreak and took myself a nap in some thick trees on a hill top. I woke up around noon, chewed on some dried beef, and watered the horses from a bucket. I gave my prisoner a drink of water, too. I never asked him his name because I didn't care to know. I just did my job.

The man asked me for something to eat and I told him to go to Hell.

"I wasn't told to feed you, just bring you in for a trial," I said.

The man got to begging me to relieve himself.

"Just pee your pants," I told him.

We reached Fort Smith four days later without any more trouble. I unloaded my prisoner in front of the courthouse. His pants were wet and he smelled to high heaven.

Judge Parker was watching and saw the shotgun tied on the man's back, still cocked and the string tied to the triggers. "Ain't you afraid it might go off?" the judge asked me.

I just yanked on the string and we heard a loud click. "I never bothered to load the gun," I said. "I was just running a bluff." The judge got a good laugh out of that.

"Where did you get the extra horses and guns?" he asked.

"I took them away from some friends of his and left them resting by a creek," was all I said. I sold the horses and saddles to the man at the livery barn and got fifteen hundred dollars for them. Not a bad pay day.

"I think I'll add a room to my house," I thought as I rode out of town. "Maybe two, with a bigger kitchen and a fire place. And a covered porch would be nice. With a rocking chair. And I might even buy myself a fishing pole."

I worked on my house for nearly a month before I got word from Parker that I was needed in the Nations and to come see him.

Chapter Five

Back to the Nations. The judge told me that I would not have to use my buggy with the jail on it.

"It's just some braves that jumped off the Reservation and are raiding some homesteads out west. Help catch the young, warring men, and bring them back to the Reservation Police," the judge told me.

"What if they've killed settlers?" I asked.

"If they kill an Indian, leave them alone. If they kill a white or black man, they're open game. Do as you please with them. Hang them, shoot them, I don't care," the judge said. "They're Indians and I can't hang an Indian on my gallows."

Parker showed me a map and explained that the Indians in question were from the Osage Reservation at Pawhuska. The tribe had been only three thousand strong n 1865 when they were moved from Kansas to new land in the Indian Territory. Feared by the other tribes, most of them stood over six feet tall and were very war-like. Some of the younger ones left their new Reservation and were burning some white settler's farms on farther west.

"See if you can find them," said the judge. "Contact the Osage Indian agent at Pawhuska. I have no idea what his name is, just find out when you get there."

I wandered around for two weeks before I found a trading post just east of the Arkansas River, with Indian allotment supplies. The man running the post was named Will Smith. I introduced myself to Mr. Smith and asked him about the Osage Indian agent, who he was and where I could find him.

"Good luck," said Smith. "When the Army brought the allotment money around the first of last month, as soon as they left, he stole the money and headed back east. I believe his name was Bert Spears. Short, skinny feller with a bald head. Looks flushed all the time."

"What do you mean, flushed?" I asked.

"Red faced or ruddy colored all the time," Smith offered. "It won't be too hard to find him, he's traveling with his wife. She's a tall, red-headed woman who dresses rather fancy for this part of the country."

"Allotment money?" I asked. "What was it for?"

"The Indians get paid on the first of the month to buy supplies," Smith explained. "With no money, they can't buy anything in my store. There's no credit allowed to them. The Indians will go hungry. It's either hunt for game or starve. That's when a bunch of the younger ones left, stole some horses from the other tribes and headed west is all I know."

"Which way were this Bert Spears and his wife headed?" I asked.

"The closest town with a hotel is northeast of here in Kansas," Will answered. "I believe they call it Coffeeville. It's not too far from here."

"How long ago did Spears leave?" I asked him.

"Must be going on two weeks now," said Will. "I'm betting he's still there in Coffeeville. He's got to come back and collect another allotment next month on the first and that's only a week away."

"How's the money paid?"

"Like me," said Smith, "most trading post don't like gold. Too much money in one place. Silver is easier for the Indian's to understand. They can't get it through their heads how paper money works."

"I think I'll hang around," I said, "and wait on this Bert Spears. If you see him before I do, don't let on I'm around. I'll see if I can find myself a teepee to live in for a spell."

I bought myself some new blankets, pans, and ten pounds of jerked and dried beef. It only took me an hour to find a young squaw with a teepee that was happy to let me move in for a spell. There was running water just outside the door, and plenty of fire wood.

I asked the young squaw about the allotment money. She said they hadn't received any for over two months, and that nearly everyone was out of silver.

Two days before the first of the month, I saw an Army regiment come by the teepees. I got on my horse and rode to the trading post. I found a Sergeant Ward, the one in charge, and told him who I was and asked if we could talk in private. I explained to him about Bert Spears stealing the allotment money and taking out for Kansas. Coffeeville, I believed. I told the sergeant I was going to arrest Spears for theft of government funds and take him back to Judge Parker in Arkansas.

"The hanging judge?" Ward asked.

"That's the one," I said.

"Good enough for me," the sergeant said. "Who would you recommend for the new Indian agent for the Osage?"

"Will Smith," I answered without hesitation. "I believe him to be an honest man and he knows I'll check up on him."

Sergeant Ward had Smith to sign off for the Indian Allotment money.

"I will be checking up on you," I told Smith. "I'm going after this Bert Spears now."

I left and headed north on the trail to Coffeeville, Kansas. I was taking my time, in no hurry, and thinking that maybe I would meet up with this Bert Spears and his red-headed wife on the trail back south.

I camped that night in some cottonwood trees that were as thick as hair on a dog's back and not too far off the trail. I was fixing coffee the next morning when, I guess, Bert smelled my campfire and coffee boiling. He drove his buggy right up to me and asked if he could share in some hot coffee.

"What brings you out to Osage country?" Bert asked after he saw my badge.

I never said a word, just let him my cup of hot coffee with my right hand. As soon as he took the cup, I hit him as hard as I could with a roundhouse left and knocked him out cold. The red-headed woman started screaming. She must have thought I was after her. She jumped out of the buggy and started running up the trail. I just let her go. After all, I wasn't after her.

I tied my shotgun up under and around Bert's neck with a short belt run through the rings at the end of the barrel. I ran his belt through the trigger guard and tied the stock to him in front so that the butt was between his legs. Then I handcuffed him with his hands behind him, took a short rope and tied him upright in the seat. Then I finished my breakfast before he woke up.

Bert came to and realized he was tied up. He started cussing at me and looking around. He saw the shotgun tied up under his neck.

"Is this thing loaded?" he asked, his eyes wide with shock.

"Yes," I told him, "and both hammers are cocked, with a string tied to them triggers."

"What are you going to do to me?" he asked.

"I'm going to take you back to Fort Smith to see Judge Parker for stealing the Allotment money from the Osage Indian tribe," I told him.

"But, I didn't take all of it," he sniffled. "They've still got some left."

"I don't give a damn if you only stole a dollar," I told him. "You're still going to see Judge Parker."

"Where is my wife?" Bert asked.

"She was headed north as fast as she could run," I said. "How far back is it to Coffeeville?"

"About ten miles," Bert replied.

"Well," I said, "she will make it back before dark."

With that over, I headed out for Fort Smith. I just tied my horse on to the tailboard of Bert's buggy, with him griping about his hands being tied behind his back. I just blocked him out and looked at the scenery. I kind of liked the color in the trees. It was getting on close to fall and we'd already had a frost.

Judge Parker was surprised to see me at the courthouse steps one morning with a prisoner. It took me close to half a day, writing up the charges on Bert Spears for stealing the allotment money from the Osage tribe. I'd found out it was a Federal offense and the only one

Judge Parker ever got to try. And, it got me a ten dollar a month raise.

I just kept Bert's buggy, stored it in my barn along with the one I'd made a jail on. I turned his horse loose in my corral.

Judge Parker made me stay and testify at Bert's trial. I don't know why, seeing as how the judge was going to hang him anyway with or without my testimony. The judge decided to have the hanging that coming Saturday morning when there were more people in town. As soon as the hanging was over, Judge Parker told me I still needed to catch them braves that had left their Reservation.

So, there I was, still chasing after a bunch of young braves on the far west side of the Reservation. Close to Anadarko, I came upon a farm house along the east banks of the Wichita River. It was all burned out. The family was in the yard, all scalped and mutilated. It was a man, woman, and a young boy around ten I would say. I spent the evening and part of the next day getting them underground, or what was left of them anyway.

I wrote the whole scene down in a ledger and drew some pictures for the judge. I searched the grounds and what was left of the farmhouse, looking for their names, but I didn't find anything. I did learn from looking around, that the Indians had walked to the homestead. There were just four in all and they had taken four horses when they left, all shod ponies. That was uncommon for an Indian to ride a horse with shoes, but when you steal them, I guess it doesn't matter.

I trailed the Indians for a week before I came upon a cattle drive with about the biggest bunch of longhorn cattle I had ever seen. They were all gathered together just about a mile on past the North Canadian Riverbed. It was early in the morning and the cowboys were having coffee and bacon at the chuck wagon fire, along with some dried bread. The way it looked, they had plenty of coffee.

I just rode up and asked if I could share some of their coffee. One man told me his name was Charles Goodnight. Another's name was Joe Tolbert, and he acted very nervous around me for some reason. The others were Shorty Hawk and Billy Bours, the cook. The other cowboys were already working the herd back together after a night of grazing.

I walked to my saddle bags and got my cup, the n filled it to the brim, taking my time and listening to a story about the Indians they had tied to the big wheels on the rear of their wagon. I learned there was four of them to start with, but were down to only two after raiding their cook's wagon the night before. The Indians were caught trying to steal some jerked beef the cook had stored for wet days when they couldn't have a fire.

Goodnight said they killed two of them right off and chased the other two down. The two Indians were roped and dragged back to the wagon. I finally told them I was a U.S. Marshal out of Fort Smith and that I had been tracking the Indians they'd caught for over a week. I also told them about the family the Indians had killed and scalped down south of there a ways on the Wichita River.

I finished my coffee and biscuit, walked over and looked at the ones tied on the big wheels and the other two piled a ways off. Goodnight told me they were trying to make up their minds as to what to do with them, just shoot them or hang them, when I rode up.

"If you don't mind," said Goodnight, "we'll leave that up to you."

I just asked the cook, Billy, if I could borrow his wagon for a short drive.

"Sure, just don't run off with mules," was all Billy said.

I told him okay, then climbed in the seat and released the brake. I took off with the mules at a fast walk. The two Indians were going around them wheels fast enough that when they finally came loose, they flew up in the air nearly twenty feet. I turned the wagon around and looked at them. Just a bag of bones. I put a shot in each one and brought Billy's wagon back to him.

Joe Tolbert was standing there with his mouth open, wondering what the hell had just happened. I told Goodnight to keep the horses they rode in on, there was no one left down south to claim them anyway.

"Just drive your longhorn cattle herd over them," I said. "Leave the buzzards to just rot in the sun after what they did to that family down south."

I rode back south toward Anadarko.

Chapter Six

As I was riding back to Anadarko along the Wichita River bottoms, I came across some cowboys early in the morning. They were all having coffee and dried out biscuits. They had six Indians tied to some tree limbs and seven more piled up, dead. I was wondering what had gone on so I introduced myself.

The Indians looked to be Osage, taller than most tribes in the Territory. A man by the name of John Chisholm and his cow hands, a trail drive outfit heading south after delivering a herd of longhorns to Abilene, Kansas, were heading back home to his ranch at Mineral Wells, Texas.

Chisholm told me they had come across a family that had been killed and all the buildings burned out, with some parts of the corral still left standing. There were two men and woman, all scalped, lying in the yard. He said that after looking the homestead over, they realized the Indians had taken a small girl with them after the raid. John said they'd found small tracks in the yard and a doll with a blue dress on.

"The whole thing looked to be homemade," Chisholm recalled, "and fairly new-looking."

That had been up somewhere on the north Canadian River a day ago. Chisholm and his men had trailed the Indians, raided their camp the night before as the savages were poking the child with sharp sticks for entertainment.

"We killed several of the Indians," John said, "and tied the rest of them up in the trees. We've been wondering what to do with them ever since we rescued the child. I can't make up my mind whether to hang them or just shoot them after what they was doing to the little girl and her family."

The child looked to be around five, I would guess. Chisholm showed the little girl to me.

"Okay," I told John, "I will take care of the rest of them savages." I walked over to the first one in line, staring him right in the face. The Indian was defiant and tried to spit on me and was calling me bad names. I told the men to start turning the dead Indians over on their bellies. Seeing that done, the Indian started wailing out loud.

"What does that mean?" Chisholm asked, "turning them on their bellies?"

"It means they're not now, nor ever, going to their happy hunting grounds."

I shot the first one between the eyes and cut him loose, then rolled him onto his belly. The wailing got louder as I went down the line. Then, when I was finished, I told the cowboys to leave the Indians like they were, on their bellies.

"I'll tell the Indian Agent at Anadarko where they're at," I told John Chisholm. "I believe this is called Dead Indian Creek on the Territory maps. It's earned its name now."

The cowboys and I finished our breakfast of coffee and dried bread.

I caught a lot of flak for leaving those Indians on their bellies. Every tribe in the Territory swore to kill me for it. But Judge Parker stood behind me. I got shot at so many times I must have lost count. I must have run down at least a dozen different Indians and killed them over the next five years.

Finally, the judge made me stop going to the Territory and assigned me to just bring prisoners to court from the jail. I never had a prisoner try to escape. I would just tied that old shotgun around their necks with a belt and cock it. Of course, it was never loaded, but the prisoners never knew that. It scared the hell out of them.

Over the next several years all I did was move prisoners from the lockup to the courthouse for trial and fish in my creek. I even tried to wear out my rocking chair. I even quit carrying that old Colt.

I ran into an old friend from the orphanage one day, a man named Bob Ford. He was riding through Fort Smith with some other cowboys, a couple of brothers named James. The first thing Bob did when he saw me was to holler out "John!" as loud as he could. It was a good thing Judge Parker wasn't around to hear it.

I told Bob right quick to never call me John again, that I had to change my name when I arrived in Fort Smith.

"I changed it to Sam Bass," I told him, but I never did explain why.

We hung out for a couple of days at my cabin. When Ford told me they had to be leaving, I noticed the only gun Bob carried was an old Henry rifle. I gave Bob that old Colt of mine, and the holster.

"Be very careful where you point it," I told him, "that old gun has a tendency to go off by itself."

When Ford palmed the old Colt, he felt a tingle in his hand. He never told me about it, just rammed it down in the holster. As they rode off, Bob and the James boys, he hollered back at me.

"Sam, we're headed to Coffeeville, Missouri!" Close to a month or more later I read in a newspaper that a man named Bob Ford had shot and killed one of the James boys. Jesse James, I believe it said.

Several years later, I was getting too old to work every day so the last job I took care of for the U.S. Marshal's service was to deliver the old hanging rope that Judge Parker always used to a town out west for a hanging. I studied the new maps of Oklahoma and the Indian Territory and bought myself a round-trip ticket on the Overland Stage to the Fort Sill, Oklahoma Army post.

It took a week to get there by stage, and I rented a buggy from the livery at Fort Sill and left early one morning after breakfast, heading west to Frederick, Oklahoma. I got there in less than a day.

When I got there for the hanging, I visited with the sheriff and the judge. They left it up to me to find a place to hang the man or to build a gallows. I asked the sheriff if he had a hay barn with an upper loft and door.

"Yeah," the sheriff said, and showed it to me. It was three blocks south of the courthouse.

I checked it over and told the sheriff it would work just fine, after the trial that the town's people had started calling 'the case of the staggering horse.' It seemed a black man and his wife had been to a dance one evening and, upon arriving home, encountered a horse on their front covered porch. They scared the horse and it killed the wife, the horse stomped her to death. On further investigation, the sheriff had learned the couple had had a fight at the dance over her flirtations with another man and the husband had slapped her around some. After getting home, he finally beat her to death with an axe handle. The sheriff had found it, all covered in blood and hidden in the barn out back of the house. But, the man blamed it on a horse that was running loose. With no horse tracks in the yard, the sheriff figured out the man beat his wife to death himself.

After a short trial, the judge in Tillman County sentenced the man to hang by the neck until he was dead. Being the first hanging in the state of Oklahoma, Judge Parker had sent his rope to be used in the hanging, and sent it with me, U.S. Marshal Sam Bass, a black man, to get the job done.

Judge Parker's rope was tied to a beam above the upper door of the hay barn. The black man had been sentenced to hang by the neck until he was dead. Me, being black myself, on the day of the hanging, I just tied my old shotgun with a belt around the condemned man's neck, handcuffed him, and marched him from the jail all the way down to the hay barn. Nearly everyone in town followed as we climbed the stairs and I tied the rope around the condemned man's neck with a bag over his head. I just pushed him out the door of the loft with Judge Parker's rope around his neck, and let him hang there for an hour. Then I let him down and the local doctor pronounced him dead. I rolled up Judge Parker's rope, placed it back in its protective canvas bag, loaded it up in the rented buggy, and left town, headed east from Frederick, Oklahoma.

Chapter Seven

After the hanging was over with, I loaded up Judge Isaac Parker's rope in the rented buggy and headed back east toward Fort Sill. It was late in the evening. I didn't want to spend the night in Frederick, Oklahoma after the hanging. There were too many of the hanged man's friends around town.

My belly was growling at me and I remembered that I hadn't eaten anything after breakfast. It was late in the day, so I stopped in a small town just east of Frederick, around ten miles or so. It was a little village that called itself Hollister, Oklahoma. I saw a café just across from the bank, but noticed the bank was the only place in town that had a water trough that was full. With no water pump in sight, I tied the rig up right there in front of the bank.

As I was doing this, I noticed through the window, that someone had left the vault doors open. I could see several stacks of money just sitting there. I thought someone was still in the bank working and thought nothing more of it.

I walked across the street to the café, found myself a table in the very back of the room, and ordered my meal. I was trying not to bother anyone. The only other men in there was the banker and maybe his teller, talking about the day's business.

I overheard the banker saying to the teller, "Well, we're closed for the day and all locked up. I'll see you in the morning."

I wasn't bothering anyone, just having my meal. The banker saw me and told the owner of the café, "If I ever see a black man in here again, I will call your note in and you can either pay up or get the hell out of Hollister, Oklahoma."

I heard all this and was thinking to myself, "this banker is a real nice fellow. I would like to do some business with him sometime."

I was finished anyway, so I just paid up and left. I walked back over to the buggy and left Hollister, Oklahoma behind.

An old, red dirt street curved around to the south, circled around and went back behind the bank. There were no other buildings or houses in sight, just open prairie grass and the sun setting on to the west. I stopped the buggy and sat there a while. Then, I made up my mind to improve upon my retirement funds. I loosely tied the buggy's horse to a rail behind the bank and forced the back door in. It was just a wooden frame door. I put my shoulder on one side, and my foot on the other, and spread the door frame enough so that the lock popped open.

The sun was just setting in the west and horizon looked red with a pan-sized sun just going down. It was real pretty, I thought. It was nearly dark and the sun setting in the west meant that anybody looking into the bank windows from across the street could not see anything inside. The banker was standing on the boardwalk looking at the bank's windows from across the street and saw a flash of red as I came in the back door and closed it.

Just as I had sacked up all the money from the unlocked safe, shots rang out and one of the windows flew out of the front of the bank. It just so happened there was a gun and shells in the safe. I grabbed it and started firing back at the banker and his teller across the street.

We shot back and forth at each other for an hour or more. The streets were dark with no moon and no street lights, the only light was from the guns we were firing at each other. When I ran out of bullets, I threw the old gun into the safe and closed the door. I spun the dial, locking it.

I just took my sack of money and walked out the back door, pulled it to, and left, headed northeast to Fort Sill Army post, walking the horse real slow. I could still hear the men firing shots into the bank and I was over a half mile off to the north when I decided to have some more fun. I threw the money sack in with the Judge's rope and tied the canvas back tight. I put on a canvas duster that came with the buggy. I ran that buggy horse all the way back to Hollister, Oklahoma, making all the noise I possibly could. I stopped just short of the café, dumped a box of shotgun shells into a coat pocket and stomped all the way to the men who were still shooting into the bank.

I, U.S. Marshal Sam Bass, made quite a sight and a lot of noise in the dark with that big old white duster swinging back and forth. I hollered out, "What's going on there?"

The banker saw the badge on my shirt and said, "We're being robbed, Marshal!"

I had my old double barrel ten gauge shotgun loaded up with double ought buckshot and a pocket full of shells. I just pulled both triggers at the same time and blew out a big window from across the street. Then, I ran into the middle of the street, loaded up my shotgun again, and shot out another big window. I loaded up once more and blew the whole front door off the hinges, right on into the bank.

I ran into the bank, loaded again, and shot into a corner. I did the same thing at a big desk, blew it all to pieces. Wood and chair and papers were flying across the room. Then I reloaded and blew the whole back door off the frame and all out into the back yard. I ran out into the place where I'd parked before and stomped all over my tracks. I pulled both triggers toward the south and told the banker I saw them and thought they were headed to Loveland, Oklahoma. That was a small town southeast of Hollister about seven miles away that I remembered seeing on the map I'd studied back in Fort Smith.

"It looks like they got away," I told the banker. "You better ride to Frederick and get the Tillman County sheriff to chase them down. I've got to get back to Fort Smith with Judge Parker's hanging rope or he will have my hide tanned."

With that said, I left, headed to Fort Sill, Oklahoma.

The banker told his teller to get the Tillman County sheriff and took off south toward Loveland himself on a horse. He rode all the way there and back with no bank robbers in sight. By doing so, he had covered up any tracks the outlaws would have made.

The sheriff couldn't find any tracks the next day that weren't old. Between the banker and the teller, along with the U.S. Marshal, they had covered up any tracks the robbers might have made. The 'outlaws' got away. The bank was a total loss. There was nothing left to salvage except the vault and it was empty.

I made the Overland Stagecoach ride back to Fort Smith, Arkansas. I cleaned out the money from the canvas sack and hid it in my cabin, then delivered Judge Parker's rope back to him early the next morning.

"I'm retiring," I told the judge. "I'm just going to fish every day from now on."

Parker asked me if I had managed to save up enough money to get by in my golden years.

"Yes, I believe I can get by," I told the judge. "I've got a good buggy stored in the barn, a horse in the corral, and a creek to fish in."

The End